Alien Inspection

Cher Louise Jones

To receive news of upcoming publications, as well as
some great creative writing ideas, please visit
www.cherjones.co.uk and join the mailing list.

For Poppy

I can't wait to see the amazing things you will do.

Table of Contents

The Unexpected Visitor

'Am I late?'

Mac slammed the lid shut, trapping the voice inside. He stepped backwards and bumped into a woman pushing a whining toddler in a trolley. She stopped trying to ram a dummy into its mouth long enough to shoot Mac an evil stare. Mac ignored her and turned to the freezer cabinet.

Come on, Mac, he told himself. *It wasn't real.*

He stood on tiptoes and strained to look inside but could not see anything through the fogged glass. After all, there was nothing to see, was there? If his friends could see him, cowering away from a freezer full of potato products, he'd never hear the end of it.

'Walter, will you hurry up with those chips!' his mother called to him from the end of the aisle.

'My name is Mac!'

Well, technically, it *was* Walter. Walter McKenzie. He was named after his grandfather. Walter couldn't remember much about him, but he bet he'd hated the

1

name, too. He sometimes imagined that, had he been there, his grandfather would have stood up at Mac's christening, when the vicar asked if there were any objections (does that happen at christenings or just at weddings?) and declared that he would not allow yet another child to be saddled with such an awful name.

Walter had tried to fix the giant cosmic mistake that had been his name by calling himself Mac. The problem was that hardly anybody else did.

'I can't hear a word you're saying, Walter. And please don't yell,' his mother yelled.

Mac took a tentative step forward, then another. At last, he was peering into the misty glass of the freezer lid. He saw nothing. He moved his face closer until the tip of his nose felt numb from the cold, and his nostrils left round clouds of condensation.

'Walter, get a move on!' His mother's voice was becoming shrill, a sure sign that the endless queues and the fight with the old lady over the last pack of frozen sprouts had pushed her to her limit.

Come on, Mac, pull yourself together, he told himself. *It was just your imagination.* But as his face neared it, the lid to the freezer shuddered, as if somebody were banging on its underside.

'What are you doing?'

Mac looked up to see his mum standing, with her hands on her hips, before him.

'I…I…' Mac couldn't find the right words to explain what he had seen.

'If you want something done…' his mother muttered as she marched towards the freezer.

'Mum, wait…'

The lid opened with a groan, and Mac's mother leant over, reaching deep inside. Mac squeezed his eyes shut, waiting for her scream to bounce around the aisle.

'Walter, they're right here.'

Mac opened first one eye, then the other, to find his mother holding a bag of chips triumphantly in front of him.

'Honestly, sometimes it's like you can't see what you are looking for unless it grows teeth and bites you.'

A shudder ran through him as he thought about what a real possibility that had been. He watched as his mother made her way to the trolley and dropped in the bag of chips.

Mac was tempted to follow her. In fact, his feet, which seemed to have more sense than his brain, turned in her direction and began to walk.

But then, Mac thought, *who would believe me?* He needed proof.

Mac noticed a discarded crate on the other side of the aisle. He grabbed it and placed it opposite the freezer. Then, he hopped on top of it, making himself as tall as possible, while keeping a safe distance. Next, he reached into his pocket for his phone and flipped on his camera app. He held it out in front of him with his thumb paused over the shutter button.

As he stood craning his neck, a tentacle danced from the freezer as if under a snake charmer's spell. Coiled within its grasp was a bag of frozen spuds.

In his panic, Mac lost his footing and tumbled off the crate. He lay sprawled on the floor while the green limb waved in the air above him.

'This simply cannot be right!'

The voice was posh, each syllable carefully pronounced. Like a newsreader. Or the Queen. Only it was a man's voice. At least, Mac thought so.

Mac scooted backwards on his bottom until he was sat with his back pressed against the cabinet. He stayed like that for several minutes, listening to the huffing and tutting coming from across the aisle.

Finally, Mac's curiosity got the better of him and he scrambled to his feet. Then he took a step forward, and another, until he was looking down on the strangest creature he had ever seen. Its skin was rubbery, like a dolphin, but shimmered green as he moved. Where there should have been arms and legs, suckered tentacles danced and waved. Two knobs, like

5

those on an old-fashioned radio, sat on either side of its forehead.

'Is this right?' the creature asked, thrusting the potatoes towards Mac, with its one eye bulging.

'Right?' He examined the packaging for any clues.

'This says the date is November 2020.'

'And?'

The creature slapped its tentacle against its forehead. 'Is that the correct date?' He sounded out each word as though Mac were an imbecile.

Give me a break, Mac thought. *It isn't every day that you find a monster sitting in the freezer cabinet at your local supermarket.*

'Oh, no. That's the sell-by-date.' Having never met a monster before, Mac had nothing to compare his reaction to, but he was certain he saw the creature's frantic form slump with relief. 'No, it's June.'

'What? So, it is 2020? My goodness, what must you think of me?' The creature's limbs were flapping again, each moving like they were pedalling an invisible bicycle. Mac backed away, not wanting to get on the wrong side of a monster hissy fit.

'Well,' the creature sighed as he turned his bulbous eye toward Mac. 'I can only apologise for my tardiness.'

Mac searched around him. Finally, he poked his finger to his own chest. 'To me?'

'Who else? I assure you that I am usually a very punctual **Zergonian**. It must have been the detour at the Milky Way that did it. The meteor showers we've been having this decade have been playing havoc with the **zip way**s.'

Mac was sure he saw the glimmering green/grey of the creature's skin blush purple.

An alien, then, Mac thought. *Not a monster at all.*

'Is that your name? Zergonian?'

'Not unless your name is human?' the creature answered, his tone more than a little curt. 'Surely, you were told my name when you were given this assignment?'

The Zergonian sighed as the same blank look crept across Mac's features.

'Assignment?'

'You mean you haven't been sent by the Council of Zergonian Inspectors?'

'Council of Ze…?'

'Or COZI, as they are known for short. Oh dear, this is most strange. An agent was supposed to meet me here and guide me as I filled in my report. But then, I am late; maybe they assumed the inspection was cancelled.'

A tentacle reached up and scratched the thick red skin that stuck from the top of the creature's head like a Mohican.

'But we must proceed. Zergonian scientists visit your planet all the time, but a full inspection has not been carried out for decades. The inspection is supposed to be carried out every **zet**, that's twenty years to you, and this planet is past due.'

'Maybe you got the wrong place,' Mac suggested. 'You do realise that this is a supermarket, don't you?'

His thick green eyelid blinked, one, two, three times, as the Zergonian stared at Mac. Then the creature threw back its head and opened its mouth in a cavernous belly laugh (though Mac wasn't convinced that this football with tentacles had a belly). As Mac peered into the inky black of the alien's mouth, past the toothless gums and over the yellow tongue, he could see an endless black space where stardust danced in hypnotic swirls and planets collided.

'You humans are worth keeping just for the comedy value. This has been the official meeting place for COZI for thousands of years. Do you think, in all that time, that it has always been your local supermarket?' He raised his single eyebrow above his hooded eye. 'Well, I guess you will have to do. I am Zalot of **Zergon,** and I have come to inspect your planet.'

'Oh, OK. I'm Mac. Nice to meet you, I guess.' Mac began to stretch out a hand for Zalot to shake but then decided against it.

'Well, we have no time to waste,' Zalot said. 'Let's get this tour started.'

'Hang on a minute; I'm not a guide. I wouldn't know how!'

'You live here, do you not?' Zalot took Mac's silence as a yes. 'Then, you will do fine.'

'I can't,' Mac insisted. 'I have school work and football practise; I really can't fit an alien tour into my schedule.'

'But you must…'

Zalot began to rise, using his six limbs to push his plump body up and out of the cabinet.

'Walter! Walter, where are you?' His mother's voice floated above the aisles.

'That's my mum. I have to go now. I hope you find the person you are looking for.' Mac dropped the freezer lid down with a thump.

As he ran towards his mother's voice, he could hear the muffled yelps of one very angry alien coming from inside.

The Way of the Dinosaurs

By the next morning, Mac had all but convinced himself that the encounter in the supermarket had been a dream.

It was when he lifted the lid to the toilet that he realised that he was not that lucky.

'I suppose you think that was funny, do you?' Zalot's voice echoed up from the bottom of the pan.

'Oh no,' Mac moaned as he pushed the flush above the toilet.

Zalot screeched with rage as he spun around and around. He clutched at the toilet seat as the whirlpool of water dragged him down. One by one, each of his tentacles popped off the seat and danced like an aquatic plant as he circled the toilet pan.

'You **zuznic**!' he yelled before disappearing into the drain. Mac had no idea what a zuznic was, but he guessed by the way Zalot had glowered at him, as his bulbous body was sucked into the sewerage system, that it was not a good thing.

'Well, that's the end of that then.' But as he went to dress for school, he couldn't shake off the feeling that it wasn't. And he was right.

As usual, his mum had hung his ironed school uniform inside his wardrobe. But there was one notable difference. A head stuck out of the collar of his shirt, and an unblinking eye was staring at him.

'Now, that was extremely rude,' Zalot snapped, covering the front of Mac's clean white shirt with flecks of blue spit.

'I'll just wear yesterday's shirt,' said Mac as he closed the wardrobe door on the disgruntled alien.

Down in the kitchen, when his mother opened the fridge, Mac tried to ignore the green limbs that fought for freedom.

'Would you like orange or apple juice?' his mother asked, oblivious to the struggle. 'Walter, are you listening to me?'

'It's Mac.'

'That's strange because I distinctly remember asking them to write 'Walter' on your birth certificate.

Besides, you should be proud to be named after such a great man.'

Walter didn't argue. They'd had the same conversation a hundred times over, and the alien trying to fight its way out of the fridge seemed a far more pressing issue. Besides, his mother's eyes welled up when she talked about her father, and he didn't like to upset her. He wished he could be as proud of his own.

'I'll stick to milk.' He reached for the jug at the centre of the table.

'You cannot ignore me forever!' Zalot yelped as the fridge door was slammed on a protruding tentacle.

'I can try,' Mac muttered under his breath. He pushed away his toast, deciding he wasn't hungry after all.

It was when he opened his school bag to put in his geography homework that Mac decided that it might be time to admit defeat. Zalot bounded from his bag, stopping a few inches from Mac's face.

'Do not think about shutting me back in,' Zalot warned, his bloated eyeball pulsing with anger. 'I have been a very patient Zergonian up until now, but you are wearing on my last **zebde**.'

Mac slumped down on the bed next to the alien, his head in his hands. 'Why don't you ask someone else to be your guide?'

Zalot opened his mouth, covering it with a tentacle in mock surprise.

'Someone else, of course! I will just ask someone else. If only I had thought of that myself. I could have saved myself the trouble of being abandoned, squashed, and flushed.'

Mac did not consider himself to be a genius, but he knew when somebody was being sarcastic with him, even if they were from another galaxy.

'Unfortunately, you are it,' Zalot continued. 'I am invisible to everyone except the first person I saw after **zorbing** in. That's why it was important that my guide was waiting for me. Instead, I got…' Zalot stopped to look Mac up and down. '…you.'

'But I'm just a kid; I am barely into double digits. What can I teach someone from another planet?'

'Teach *me*? Teach *me*, he says!' Zalot laughed. His deep chuckle went on and on and on. Mac thought, if Zalot had a waist, he would have been bent double with laughter.

Suddenly, he stopped.

'You...' Zalot stabbed a tentacle at Mac's chest. '*You* cannot teach me anything. You just need to go about your business, and I will observe.'

'And what if I say no?' He was nervous to hear the answer.

'Then,' Zalot said, his voice a whisper, 'your planet will automatically fail the inspection.'

Mac gulped. 'What does that mean?'

'It means,' Zalot explained, 'your planet will be cleaned. Wiped spotless, made sterile, taken back to basics.'

'I don't really understand,' Mac admitted.

'Why does that not surprise me?' Zalot rubbed his brow. 'You have heard of the Ice Age, haven't you? That was COZI at work. And the end of the dinosaurs? Also, us. When we believe the inhabitants have got to the point where all they can do is destroy themselves, we take action to save the planet.'

Mac let this sink in for a moment. The dinosaurs were extinct…

'But what about the people that live here?'

If he'd had shoulders, Zalot would have shrugged them. 'In my experience, they are the cause of the problem. The planet may be better off without them.'

Mac tried to imagine the Earth without people. Everybody he knew, gone. His parents, his family, his friends, his teachers… O.K, maybe he wouldn't mind his teachers being wiped out. But his family and his friends? No!

Perhaps the tears that pooled in the corners of Mac's blue eyes made the alien feel guilty because Zalot placed a tentacle on the boy's shoulder. 'But it may not come to that if you help me.'

'I guess I don't have much choice, do I?' Mac said, wiping his nose on his sleeve.

'No,' Zalot admitted, 'you do not.'

Rotten Fish Guts and Crispy Socks

'I have a geography trip today, so you will have to stay in my bag.' Mac opened his rucksack wide, ready for Zalot to climb in.

'You must be having a **zeflar**,' Zalot replied, his toothless mouth wide. 'There is no way on Zergon I am getting back in that thing. It smells funny, and I am sure whatever is living at the bottom has me labelled as lunch.'

'Well, what am I supposed to do, introduce you as my cousin Ed visiting from up North?'

'There is no need to be snippy. If you had been paying attention, you would know that no being from this planet can see me, except for you.'

'Well, I'm not sure my teacher is from this planet,' Mac said.

'Totally impossible. We have no Zergonians posing as teachers in this area. Doctors, dentists, and policemen, yes, but no teachers. Now, let's go.'

Mac plodded down the stairs, wondering if his own dentist had seemed any different at his last check-up. He paused at the bottom of the steps to yell goodbye to his mum, and then, he was out of the door.

Mac's school was a five-minute walk away, usually. But with Zalot in tow, shuffling along on rubbery tentacles, it was ten past nine by the time they reached the gates. A purple glow filled Zalot's cheeks as he heaved in deep breaths.

'Oh no! They're getting on the bus!'

Sure enough, a line of children, shepherded by a looming bird-like woman, were boarding the waiting coach. 'I'm here, Miss!' Mac called as he raced to meet his teacher, leaving Zalot toddling behind him. 'Don't leave without me!'

'Walter McKenzie, what time do you call this?' the woman asked, pointing to her watchless wrist. Not too bright, these teachers.

'Sorry, Miss Penndel, I overslept,' Mac lied. The doors hissed shut behind him.

As he made his way to the nearest seat, Mac's foot caught, and he lurched forward, winding himself on the back of the seat in front.

When Mac looked to see what he had tripped over, he found a foot sticking out into the aisle.

'My bad,' Ryan said, holding his hands out in defence. Then he and his friends broke into peals of laughter.

'Will you stop messing around and get to your seat, Walter,' Miss Pendell said.

Walter sank into the mildew scented upholstery. He replayed the scene with Ryan as he did every time that he encountered the school bully. He supposed the sensible thing would have been to tell Miss Pendell. But Mac worried that people would call him a snitch.

Perhaps he should have confronted Ryan. Maybe they would have fought. Mac daydreamed about the rest of the class chanting his name as he wrestled Ryan into a headlock. However, in the scenario that played in his head, Ryan was not a foot taller than him and didn't have his gang of minions to back him up.

Mac leaned back in his seat and tried not to think about it. Then, he saw Zalot glaring at him from the pavement. Mac sat bolt upright. He couldn't let Earth fail its inspection just because he had wanted to take a trip to a farm.

'Miss, I left my lunch at home,' he called. 'I need to go back for it.'

'Well,' snorted Miss Penndel, 'you will have to share mine. You are a lucky boy, it's Tuesday, and that's pickled egg and tuna day.'

Mac's stomach gave a gurgle of protest. 'Really, Miss…'

'Enough!' yelled Miss Penndel, signalling to the driver to start the engine.

Now, in the brief time that Mac had known Zalot, he had learned that he was nothing if not persistent, an opinion that the Zergonian was about to confirm again. Approaching the bus window, Zalot extended a tentacle and gave it a tap. Mac scanned the seats around him, wondering if anybody had heard, but the other children were chattering away about what they were going to see on the farm. Zalot tapped the glass again before breaking out into a gummy grin.

What happened next turned Mac's stomach even more than the image of Miss Penndel's pickled egg and tuna sandwiches. Zalot opened his mouth wide and stuck himself to the window like a sucker on a stuffed toy. Then gradually, using his tentacles as leverage, he edged himself higher and higher towards the small open window above Mac's seat. A trail of blue saliva stained the glass behind him.

'Hey Mac, glad you made it.' Drew flopped down into the seat next to him.

Drew's name was actually Andrew. But when Mac had dropped Walter, Andrew had decided to call himself Drew in support. Neither name had caught on, and the only people to use them were each other.

'Did you see the match last night? Amazing.'

Mac nodded, unable to tear his eyes away from the progress of the alien, sliming his way up his window. The coach pulled away from the pavement with the alien still stuck firmly to the glass.

'I can't say I want to be a farmer when I grow up, but if it gets us out of maths, I'm not going to complain.'

The bus screeched around a corner, the driver keen to offload his cargo of screaming Year Five children. Mac was afraid Zalot would lose his grip. However, the alien just muttered under his breath before continuing his path up the pane of glass.

'Earth to Mac!' Drew called, waving a hand in front of his friend's eyes.

'Yeah, you want to be a farmer, that's great,' Mac said with his eyes fixed on the Zergonian.

Zalot had reached the top and was pushing each tentacle through the small window, one at a time. Mac could see by the way he seized the edge of the glass that he intended to catapult himself through the tiny opening and into the bus. But his plan hit a problem when he became wedged in the slender rectangle.

'Ugh, too much **zapna**,' Zalot grumbled as he tried to heave himself through. Finally, he landed on Mac's lap with a plop. 'I cannot believe you left me!' he yelled. 'What am I saying? Of course, I can believe it. You have been trying to get rid of me…'

'Mac, are you ok?' Drew asked.

Mac looked from Drew to the grumbling alien whining in his lap and back again. 'Me? Yes, I'm fine.'

'OK,' Drew said as he took out a magazine and started to read.

'And what is he doing in my seat?' Zalot flapped a tentacle towards Drew.

'It's not your seat,' Mac whispered.

'Did you say something?' Drew frowned at him.

'Not a word,' Mac replied as he tried to dodge Zalot's waving limbs without looking insane.

'I am not riding on your lap all the way to this farm place. Get him out of my seat. Or I will.'

There was a glint in Zalot's eye that Mac did not like. But what could he do; explain to Drew that an invisible alien needed his seat?

'Have it your way.' Zalot smiled.

What came next is difficult to explain, especially as Mac was the only one to see what happened, and he couldn't see much through the tears stinging his eyes. First, there came an innocent 'parf' sound, which was followed by a strange orange mist. Then came the smell; the vilest most putrid smell Mac could ever imagine. Rotten fish guts, crispy socks and ripe babies' nappies all smelt like freshly baked bread compared to this smell. All about him, Mac could hear the retching of his classmates as they breathed in Zalot's foul bottom burp.

Drew unclipped his seatbelt. 'I think Miss Penndel is calling me.' He gagged as he ran toward the front of the bus.

Zalot flashed a satisfied grin as he stretched out his six limbs in the seat next to Mac. 'I said they couldn't see me, not that they couldn't smell me.'

Spies Amongst Us

The rest of the journey to the farm was a lonely one for Mac. Zalot sat sulking in his seat, miffed that he had been abandoned yet again. None of the other children would come close because of Zalot's putrid scent. Mac was relieved when the bus bumped up the dirt track leading to the farm.

As they stepped off the coach, Mac breathed in a huge lungful of country air. The smell of manure was refreshing compared to the air on the bus.

'Follow me, children. Keep up!' yelled Miss Penndel as she marched towards the farmhouse.

'Come on Zalot; we don't want to get left behind.' But Zalot wasn't listening to Mac. He was staring at a barn in the distance.

'That is where I want to go.' Zalot pointed a green limb.

Mac stood, torn between following the alien and catching up with his class. It took just a few strides to reach Zalot, once he had made his decision.

'That's where they keep the animals,' Mac told him. 'You won't learn anything about humans there.'

'You would be surprised,' Zalot said.

Inside the barn, it was dark and damp. Pieces of lint chased one another in the beams of sunlight entering through the broken roof. Animals stood in their stalls, some chewing wearily on hay.

A cat crawled across the dusty floor, stalking some unseen prey. Occasionally, it would pounce, before lifting a paw in disappointment as it realised it had missed its invisible target.

'Yes, this is who I need to speak to.' Zalot hobbled past the stalls.

Mac tried to suppress his smile. 'Um, Zalot, animals can't talk.' Then he reconsidered, thinking of all the times he had heard birds calling to one another in the trees or dogs sniffing one another's butts at the park. 'Well, not in the same way that we talk anyway.'

'We? I cannot speak Earthling any more than you can speak Zergonian. My **zanbot** deals with that problem. It translates the languages of anyone nearby so that we can all understand one another.' Zalot held up one of his many tentacles to show Mac the thin silver band upon it. 'But that is beside the point; I am not here to speak to your farm animals.'

The cat stopped his hunt and stared before sauntering towards them and rubbing against Zalot's stumpy body.

'It can see you!' Mac cried.

'Of course,' Zalot replied as he reached down to scratch the moggy behind the ears.

'But you said no other beings but me could see you.'

'No, I said no other beings from this planet could see me but you. Cats are not from Earth,' Zalot explained, rolling his eye at the boy's stupidity.

'Of course, they are. Cats have always been here. I have a cat of my own. Well, he lives with my dad now. But I visit him all the time.'

Actually, Mac hadn't seen his dad or his cat for months. His dad had remarried and had a new baby to look after. Mac told himself he wasn't bothered. He did miss his cat, though.

'Cats have been here since *you* can remember. But COZI introduced them as spies to your planet long ago. The Egyptians knew; they worshipped them. Sensibly so, if you ask me, considering the power their feline neighbours wielded.'

Mac thought about the last museum trip his mum had forced him on. He remembered seeing statues of the Egyptian Gods, and he was sure one of them had been a cat. It was called Bastet, or something like that.

'In fact,' Zalot continued, 'we have planted cats as spies on every planet in this galaxy. Go to Mars, and you will find cats; Venus, more cats. Think about it. Do cats behave like any other animal you know? Do they sometimes seem to see things that you cannot?'

Mac thought of all those times his own cat Ninja (named for being completely black and, well, ninja-like) had chased invisible mice or meowed at something that wasn't there.

'But cats are a terrible choice of animal to use as spies!' Mac said. 'They are selfish, superior and they only care about getting fed.'

'I object to that.'

The voice wasn't Zalot's. Mac scanned the barn for whoever had spoken. 'Down here.' Mac peered down to find the tabby cat staring up at him.

'You can talk!' Mac felt light-headed.

'Obviously,' the cat replied with a sniff. 'You can't go throwing insults around. Not all of us cats are like that. I'm a working cat. I spend day after day in this barn catching mice. And this is the thanks I get.'

'I...I'm sorry. I meant no offence.'

'Hmph,' the cat replied, sticking its nose up in the air and swishing its tail as it walked away.

'Please, ignore my companion.' Zalot followed the cat. 'It is time for Earth's inspection. Could you tell me how humans treat the animals they share this planet with?'

The cat's ears pricked up at this, and Mac couldn't help suspecting that the moggy was glad of the opportunity for revenge.

'Terribly, just terribly,' the cat said. 'They eat other animals for a start.'

'So do you!' Mac protested. 'Cats eat meat as well!'

'That's true,' the cat nodded as he licked his paw. 'But the difference is we hunt for what we eat. Either that or we are given it by you humans. What we don't do is keep animals prisoner until we want to use their meat. Take the chickens on some of these farms; they are force-fed until they are so fat that they can't walk, stuffed into cages, and served up for Sunday lunch. I mean, the farmer here is better. He lets his chickens roam free. I wouldn't work for one of those barbarians, but there are plenty of them out there.'

Zalot was nodding, his tentacle to his mouth as he considered the cat's words.

'But not every human agrees with that,' Mac said. 'Take this trip today. We are here to learn all about how to keep animals safe and happy.'

'Both interesting points.' Zalot waved his tentacle. The light in the room swirled around his limb before settling to form a list, not on paper, but floating in the air in front of them. Mac put out his hand to touch it before pulling it back, worried the glowing image might burn him. 'This is the checklist that Earth must pass. There are four points: respect for other creatures, the planet, yourselves and each other.'

Mac strained to read the masses of small print at the bottom of the list, but before he could, Zalot swished his tentacle through the image, scattering it into a thousand pieces.

'It does not look as though 'point one' is going well from what this cat has told me.'

The cat gave a satisfied nod of agreement before continuing: 'And if you want to hear a real horror story, I will tell you all about my last visit to the vet. You wouldn't believe where she wanted to stick her thermometer…'

But before the tabby could continue, he was interrupted by a mysterious thud from behind them.

Mac turned to find Miss Penndel in the doorway to the barn, collapsed on the floor.

Trouble with Gas

Zalot wrapped a tentacle around Miss Penndel's ankle before beginning to drag her, unconscious, out of the barn.

'Don't hurt her!' Mac yelled as he grabbed his teacher's wrist and pulled her back, locking them in an insane game of tug of war. Miss Penndel groaned between them.

'Why would I hurt her?' Zalot dragged the teacher back towards him. 'I am just going to wipe her memory of the last few minutes.'

Mac eyed him with suspicion. 'Do that here, then.'

'If I do it here,' Zalot said, 'then your memory will be wiped too. And believe me, I don't want to risk starting afresh, persuading you to help me.'

'You said you were just going to wipe a few minutes of her memory?'

'Yes, well, the **zanolve** machine is a delicate piece of equipment, but in theory…'

'OK,' Mac said, 'I will wait outside, and you can do it in here.'

'Ha! You expect me to fall for that? Considering the number of occasions that you have tried to abandon me?'

'I won't, I promise. I want the Earth to pass the inspection. The cat can watch me if it makes you feel better.'

They both glanced over at the cat who, oblivious to their conversation, sat with its leg up in the air, licking its bottom.

'Fine,' Zalot said. 'Wait outside the door.'

Mac had been waiting a few moments when he heard it. 'Psk.'

He looked around but saw nothing.

A second later, he heard it again. 'Psk.' He saw a hand appear from around the corner of the barn, beckoning him closer with its index finger.

There he found a man dressed in a black suit. Black sunglasses covered his eyes. Even when he stood as straight as he could, Mac wasn't as high as the man's chest.

'Hi.' The man didn't respond. 'I'm Mac. What's your name?'

'That doesn't matter.'

Rude, Mac thought. But he agreed that it didn't matter as in his head he had already nicknamed him 'The Suit.'

'Were you calling me?'

'Maybe,' The Suit said.

'Well, do you want anything?'

'Perhaps.'

'Anyway,' Mac said. 'It's been lovely chatting with you, but…'

'That depends,' The Suit interrupted, 'on whether you want to save the Earth or not.'

Mac's eyes widened; he knew about Zalot and the inspection. 'Believe me; I'm trying!'

'Really?' The Suit asked. 'Because it looks to me as though you have been helping the alien.'

Mac flinched. How long had this guy been watching him?

'Yes,' Mac said. 'If I don't, we will fail their inspection, and they will wipe out the human race.'

'Is that what he told you? No, this isn't an inspection.' The Suit lifted his glasses so he could look Mac right in the eye. 'It's an invasion.'

'B-but…' Mac couldn't find the words.

'They plan to invade our planet, and you have been helping him look for the best place for their ships to land.'

'That's not true!' Mac said. 'At least I don't think it is…'

'It is. Whether you meant it or not. But you can undo the damage you have done if you help us.'

'Who is 'us'?' Mac asked.

'Global Alien Surveillance.' The Suit flicked open his wallet to show Mac his ID card but flipped it shut again before Mac had a chance to read it.

'GAS? Your department is called GAS?'

'No.' The Suit did not give a hint of a grin. 'Global. Alien. Surveillance. Do you want to help or not?'

'What would I have to do?'

'Keep doing exactly what you are doing. We'll be watching, and when it looks like he might have found a suitable location, we'll know. Simple,' The Suit explained.

'Then what?'

'Then we'll capture them all at once. Earth will be safe. You will be a hero. Though, of course, you wouldn't be able to tell anyone. It would just cause panic.'

'Hang on a minute,' Mac said as a thought occurred to him. 'You're an alien too, aren't you?'

'No, I am not.'

'Yes! You must be! Zalot said only other aliens could see him. Except for me, of course.'

'Well, if the alien said that, then it must be true.'

Mac was getting quite tired of his sarcasm.

The Suit leaned forward so that his nose was an inch from Mac's. He tapped the side of his glasses.

'Technology. They may not want us to see them, but with these, we can. Now, are you in or not? Because, believe me,' The Suit said, 'Global Alien Surveillance takes treason very seriously. And 'The Boss' hates traitors.'

The Boss? This made Mac think of the computer games he played, where the bad guy at the end of each level got bigger and scarier. The last one he'd played, 'Realms of Destruction,' had ended with a villain that had the head of a werewolf and the scales of a lizard. Just when Mac thought he had him beaten, the creature unfurled his wings and swooped on him from above.

He had woken in the middle of the night, certain that its red glowing eyes were staring at him from the gloom of his bedroom. Although he had told himself that it was just a dream, he had spent the rest of that night flinching at every whistle of the wind and creaking floorboard.

Mac swallowed hard. Whoever this 'Boss' was, he had no desire to meet him. 'Then I guess I'm in.'

Travelling in Style

'It was talking. The cat was talking,' Miss Penndel said, clutching the driver's shirt.

Mac shot Zalot a look. The alien stretched out its tentacles in defence.

'It was only my second time using the zanolve machine,' he explained. 'And the first time I tried it, the subject thought he was in pre-school after. So, it could be worse, right?'

The driver fanned a pale looking Miss Penndel with his hat. 'Of course, it was talking. And the cows were playing 'Snap!''

'You don't believe me?' The teacher's tone was strangled.

'I think you need to have a rest,' the driver told her as he snapped her seatbelt closed.

'That was close. We have to be more careful,' said Mac as Zalot jumped up onto the seat next to him.

The return journey to school was a long one. None of the excited chatter filled the coach this time.

Instead, all Mac saw were the glum faces of his classmates, disappointed by their trip being cut short.

It was not long before the lunchtime traffic piled up, and the coach crawled along. The temperature in the bus crept up as it sat in the bright June sunshine.

'What is taking so long?' Zalot moaned as he wiped away the blue sheen forming on his brow.

'We're stuck in a traffic jam. We could be here for a while,' Mac explained.

'A traffic jam? This was not mentioned in the report from the last visit.'

'Well, you said that the last inspection was done decades ago. Traffic probably wasn't such a problem back then. The more humans there are on the planet, the more cars they need.'

'Really?' Zalot had a mischievous glint in his eye. 'But humans didn't walk everywhere before the car was invented, did they? How did they travel great distances back then?'

Mac shrugged. 'Well, they rode animals, I guess.'

'Animals,' Zalot repeated. 'Tell me, Mac, do they teach you about **zene** particles in school?'

Mac shook his head.

With a flick of a tentacle, a glowing orb appeared in the air before Zalot. He coiled one of his limbs around it. 'Zene particles can be used to alter the actions, makeup, and existence of anything. You just have to focus on the change you want to make in the world.'

'Huh?' Mac's face was etched with puzzlement.

'Just watch.' Zalot threw the orb towards the ground, and it fractured, its pieces bouncing off in different directions.

Whenever they touched something, the object melted away. It reminded Mac of sitting in his mother's car in the winter as she sprayed the windscreen with de-icer. He would watch as the ice melted and twisted the appearance of the world outside; only this was happening for real.

'Stop, Zalot! What are you doing?'

'Relax,' Zalot told him. 'The effects are temporary. Zene particles act in a similar fashion to your Earth's elastic. They keep the memory of their original shape and will snap back into their previous form, eventually.'

As suddenly as it had begun, the world stopped melting and began to reshape itself. But not as it had been before. Mac watched as the seat below his friend Drew became splattered with black and white patches. Then the front stretched and curled into a head-like shape. Finally, the seat let out a very disgruntled: 'Moo!'

'A cow!' Mac cried. 'Drew is riding a cow!'

Sure enough, there sat Drew, his round glasses perched on the end of his nose and reading his football magazine, riding a cow as if nothing unusual had happened.

'Why is that strange?' Zalot chuckled. 'You are riding a goat.'

Looking down, Mac saw that he was indeed perched on a very angry goat. It bleated up at him.

All around him, people travelled along the road being carried by sheep, pigs, bulls, and every other kind of animal imaginable. Miss Penndel scooted past riding a goose. Despite the way her knees were pushed up around her ears, Mac had more sympathy for the goose.

Mac looked over his shoulder and caught sight of The Suit hanging onto the horns of a snorting bull. Occasionally, the bull would buck and dip its head, trying to throw The Suit off. But he wasn't budging. That bull had met his match.

Even from that distance and from behind dark glasses, Mac could feel The Suit's eyes boring into him. He looked away, not wanting Zalot to catch him staring.

'Zalot, you have to return it to the way it was!' Mac demanded.

'Why? You have to agree; we are moving much faster.'

Mac could not deny that the class was making great progress down the road, each oblivious to the craziness that had befallen them.

'Because this isn't the way it's supposed to be!'

'And does that mean your way is better? Just because things are as they always have been, does that mean they should stay that way?' Zalot asked from atop his beautiful black steed. Mac was not sure it was down to chance that he had ended up with the goat and Zalot the horse.

'No, but we have to find our own way to change things,' Mac said.

'Well, my way is quicker, but you do not need to worry. The zene particles will return to their original state in exactly one hour.'

Not soon enough, Mac thought as the goat bit a chunk out of his trouser leg.

Revenge of the Rubbish

Mac's whole body ached after a close encounter with an overtaking elephant. He slid down from the goat, relieved to be back at school. He was rewarded with a firm butt to his backside.

'This cannot be happening.' Mac grumbled to himself as he wrestled his backpack away from the goat.

'Well, in a short while it won't have,' Zalot said. 'Your classmates will have no memory of their adventure.'

'Lucky them.' Mac rubbed the bruise that was forming on his behind.

'We still have a while before things turn back,' Zalot said. 'Don't you want to ride your goat home?'

'I think I'll walk.'

As they made the short journey home, Mac kicked a discarded cola can down the road. It landed a few paces ahead of him with a clang before he booted it along the street again.

'What is that?' Zalot stared at the can as though it were some strange scientific specimen.

'That? Oh nothing; it's rubbish.'

'What is rubbish?' Zalot reached down to pick up the can at Mac's feet. He turned it with his tentacle before dropping it onto the floor.

'Rubbish is something that you don't want anymore. And littering is when you drop it on the ground instead of recycling it or putting it in the bin,' Mac said.

'Who picks it up?'

'I'm not sure. The local council, I suppose. And on a Thursday afternoon, I go with Mr Butcher and some kids from my class and we do litter picking in the streets near the school.'

'Oh. That does not sound very fair. Surely, people should pick up their own rubbish.'

'Yes, but that isn't how the world works.'

'Well, it should be.' Zalot had that same strange glimmer in his eye.

With a wave of his tentacle, the world became a dance of swirling colour. The tiny globes of light bounced in every direction before landing wherever there lay some rubbish. Before Mac could open his mouth to ask what was happening, a plastic bag stuck in the branches of a tree rustled into life. It stretched itself out, as if it were awakening from a deep sleep, before taking flight from the tree. It soared from the branches, its plastic wings sailing upon the breeze, before diving towards Mac and Zalot. It skimmed the top of Mac's head before rising and circling above them. Finally, it ducked out of sight behind a building.

'W…where is it going?'

'Oh, to find its owner,' Zalot explained.

'It won't hurt anyone, will it?' Mac was worried that he could be accused of being an accomplice.

'I don't think so.' Zalot scratched his head. 'Though, I have never brought rubbish to life before. But no, I think it will follow its owner until the zene particles return to normal.'

Although Zalot said this as if it were little more than an inconvenience, Mac did not fancy being one of these unlucky litterbugs.

They had moved only a few paces when a familiar figure came charging down the street towards them. Ryan was being chased by a very hungry looking hamburger container. It snapped ravenously at his heels.

'Heeeelllpppp meeeeeee!' Ryan screeched as he passed Mac. Mac did not even try to hide his grin.

A newspaper sniffed an invisible trail along the street, stopping every few paces to cock its pages against the odd lamppost or tree.

On the opposite pavement, a woman yelped as a flurry of crisp packets magnetised themselves to her skin.

'Shall we go home?' Zalot said with a yawn, bored with the chaos he had created.

'Uh-huh,' Mac nodded as the cola can at his feet hopped along the pavement. 'I think that's a good idea.'

That's when they heard it, a rumbling like a million horse hooves, all heading their way.

'Do you hear that?' Mac asked.

They both turned and stared in the direction of the approaching noise. A tsunami of rubbish faced them. Fast food wrappers, plastic bags, six-pack rings, drink bottles, all mixed to form a towering wave of waste.

'Quick!' yelled Mac as he dragged Zalot behind a tree. They stood with their backs pressed against the bark. The rubbish parted around the thick trunk, leaving them an island of safety in between.

'Look over there!' Zalot pointed to where the torrent was beginning to swirl and swell. From its depths, a whale's tail, made of thick gloopy oil, broke the surface. It towered above the tree they stood under, before disappearing into the depths.

'This is insane,' Mac said. 'We need to…'

Before he could finish, fingertips brushed his arm.

'Mmmmmaaaaaaaaccccccccc,' The Suit called as the flood of rubbish carried him along, surfing ungracefully on his bottom.

'A friend of yours?' Zalot asked.

'Nobody I recognised,' Mac lied.

As he spoke, several other men in the same dark suits, rushed past the safety of their tree. Some rode the waves, grabbing at anything they passed in an attempt to stop themselves. Others were consumed up to the waist, chest, neck, gradually being tugged under by unseen forces.

So not just 'The Suit,' Mac thought, but 'Suits.' He wasn't acting alone.

After the waves had passed, Mac pointed at the slicks of oil still covering the street. 'All of this was caused in a single year? That can't be right.'

'You are correct,' Zalot said. 'They didn't create all of this in a single year. They created it in a day.'

An Explosive Meal

Mac turned on the television and plonked himself down on the sofa.

'What's that?' Zalot asked.

'A television.' Mac weaved as he tried to see the game playing behind the alien.

'Well, obviously. Our technology is far superior to yours. We aren't restricted to these little boxes. We can interact with whatever is playing. Just last week, I was tracking herbivorous dinosaurs from your Jurassic period.'

Mac rolled his eyes. 'Good for you.'

'But still, I recognise your 'television' from the Earthling museum,' Zalot continued. 'But that wasn't what I was talking about. What are they doing?'

'Playing football.'

'Football?' Zalot adjusted one of the **zarno** knobs at his temple. His eye flickered as though he were scanning a document. 'Ah, yes, I think I have grasped the rules.'

'Good. Then you can be quiet and watch it.'

'Of course.' Zalot watched the ball pass between the players. 'So which team are you supporting?'

'Arsenal.'

'What colour are they?'

'Red.'

'Why is that man pushing …?'

'Zalot, please!'

Mac's voice had taken on a growl that Zalot didn't like. 'I'm sorry, I won't say another word.' Zalot slumped in the armchair, his tentacles draped over the arms. 'That's better. My **zenta** are killing me.'

Mac ignored him. He had been looking forward to this match all week and wanted to enjoy it in peace.

A gurgling sound echoed from the alien.

'Was that your stomach?'

'Apparently so,' Zalot said.

'Well, you know where the kitchen is. As I remember, you spent some time locked in the fridge.'

Zalot stared at Mac, unblinking. 'Too soon.'

When Zalot made his way back from the kitchen a few minutes later, every tentacle was wrapped around a different form of junk food. Chocolate bars, crisps, sweets, sausage rolls… he grasped every manner of treat.

'Is that all for you?'

'For us,' Zalot said putting the food down on the table between them. 'On Zergon we have only **zapna**. This is research.'

'You only eat one kind of food? That must be boring!' Mac's game was forgotten as he reached for one of the packets. 'This is chocolate. You have to try it.'

Zalot opened his mouth and his blue tongue snaked its way out before giving the chocolate a tiny lick. 'I like it!' he said, pulling the whole bar into his mouth.

Half an hour later, Zalot and Mac sat surrounded by empty wrappers.

'I couldn't eat another thing,' Zalot said.

'That's lucky because you ate it all.'

'Me? You ate plenty yourself,' Zalot reminded him.

'That's true. Uggghhh,' he groaned. 'I'm going to explode.'

And then they were in space — no flash of light, alien tractor beams, or black holes. One second, Mac was staring at the ceiling in his living room. The next he was staring out into an endless carpet of stars.

'Zalot! What have you done?'

Mac tried to turn and look for the alien but just managed to send himself into a somersaulting spin. It stopped when Zalot reached one of his tentacles towards Mac. When it was a couple of inches away, the space in front of him fizzed, and for the briefest moment, Mac saw the flash of a sphere encompassing him.

Once his head (and the rest of his body) had stopped spinning, Mac glared at Zalot.

'What have you done?'

Zalot didn't answer him and continued staring at him with a wide eye.

'What? Why are you looking at me like that?'

'I'm waiting for you to explode!'

'Not literally, you fool! It's a saying!'

'Oh, so I haven't saved the Earth from certain destruction?' Zalot deflated like a forgotten party balloon.

'No.' Mac spoke from between clenched teeth. 'All you've done is make me want to vomit.' That feeling didn't disappear when he looked around him. There was nothing as far as his eyes could see. The only break in the inky darkness was the pinprick stars. 'Wow.'

''Wow' indeed,' Zalot said as if he hadn't seen that view countless times before.

'Hang on. How can I talk, or breathe, if I'm in space?'

'Well, technically, you're not. You're in a **zaynap** ball, and *that* is in space. Think of yourself like a ...' Zalot twirled his tentacles as he tried to think of the word.

'Astronaut?' Mac offered. 'Explorer?'

'No, that's not it.' Suddenly, Zalot perked up. 'Hamster! Think of yourself like a hamster!'

Mac stared at him. 'Awesome.'

'Yes, it is like a giant hamster ball. It's quite easy once you get going,' Zalot said as he used all his tentacles at once to push his ball in first one direction, before making a full turn the opposite way.

Mac took a tentative step forward. Already, he missed the feel of the ground below his feet. After a few minutes stumbling in the nothingness, he'd had enough. 'Can we go back?'

Zalot raised his eyebrow. 'You're sure you are not going to explode?'

'I promise. Haven't you ever eaten too much before?'

'No,' Zalot said, 'and if you had tasted zapna, you would know why.'

'Well, we have lots of choices of food on Earth. And if you eat too much, it can make you sick, or fat, or both.'

Zalot twirled his tentacles, and just like that, they were in Mac's lounge again.

'So, choices are bad, then?'

'No, not at all. You must learn to make healthy choices. Junk food should be for a treat. Making choices is part of being human.'

'Perhaps,' said Zalot; but he looked unconvinced.

The next morning, Mac made his way down the stairs with sleepy dust sticking his eyelashes together. Zalot was gone when he woke up, and Mac felt glum, thinking he might have left without saying goodbye.

'Morning, Walter.' His mum rumpled his hair and placed his breakfast bowl in front of him.

'Mac,' he reminded her. 'Mum, what's this?' He held up a carrot with its bushy green leaves attached.

'Oh, I'm sorry, is it still dirty?' His mother ran it under the tap before plonking it back into the bowl.

'Can't I have cereal instead?' Mac stared at the offending vegetable.

His mother chuckled. 'You are in a funny mood. Now hurry up and get dressed. We have to go into the city to get you some new clothes.'

Mac dragged his feet as he went upstairs to change. Shopping was the last thing he wanted to spend his Saturday morning doing.

When he was ready, and they opened the front door to leave, Mac was surprised to find Zalot standing on the doorstep. 'Greetings, Mac.'

'Uh, yes, greetings to you, too. Where have you been?'

'Fulfilling the details of our plan,' Zalot said.

'Our plan?' A shiver travelled through Mac's body. 'What plan?'

'The plan to make this world a healthier one.' Zalot smirked. 'Look.' He raised his tentacle and pointed to the garden next door.

Mac rubbed his eyes in astonishment. His neighbour, Mr Henry, was knelt on his hands and knees, chomping on the grass from his lawn.

'Morning, Mr Henry.' Mac's mother waved as if everything was normal.

Mr Henry waved without lifting his head from his meal.

'And where are my two favourite neighbours off to today?' Mrs O'Connor struggled down the road on her walker. Bulging shopping bags were slung across her shoulders.

'Oh, Mabel, you shouldn't be carrying all that; Walter will take it.'

Mac shot his mother a glare but dutifully collected the bags from their elderly neighbour anyway. He didn't really mind; she had lived on their street for as long as he could remember and didn't seem to have any family to help her.

'Thank you, Jenny,' Mrs O'Connor said to Mac's mother. Then she turned to Mac. 'You are a lovely lad.'

Mac ducked under her arm as she reached out to pinch his cheek. 'No problem.' He hoisted the bags from the ground. 'These are heavy; what have you been buying?'

'I've been stocking up on food for Albert.' She invited Mac over to meet her cat, Albert, almost every time she saw him. He was glad she didn't invite him today; he was running out of excuses.

When he got back from loading her bags onto her doorstep, she squeezed his face between her fingers, forcing his mouth into a duck-like pout. 'You're a gem, Walt... Sorry, you prefer Mac, don't you?'

Mac grinned. 'That's right.' He suddenly liked her a whole lot more.

The journey to the train station was bizarre. People sat in trees, munching on the fruit from its branches.

They walked past Miss Penndel, who stood eating the flowers from her prize-winning rose bushes.

'I hope you are feeling better, Miss Penndel,' called Mac's mother.

'Much better, thank you.' The pink petals churned in her mouth.

When they came to the McDonalds drive-through...well, they didn't come to the McDonalds drive-through. Where there had once stood a boxy building with two huge golden arches on top, there was a vegetable patch. Customers drove up, paid their money through their window before an assistant went to the patch and pulled up a handful of root vegetables. They then handed them over, roots and dirt included.

'Zalot, what have you done?' Mac whispered. He seemed to be asking that a lot lately.

'I've done these people a favour,' Zalot said. 'Even if it is only for an hour.'

Nature Fights Back

Mac's mother marched from shop to shop, herding her son in and out of changing rooms, oblivious to the green man that trailed their every step. Zalot stared at the fashion show unfolding in front of him.

'You look great,' Jenny said.

Mac stared down at the trailing sleeves of the jumper and the trousers that pooled on the floor.

'Well, obviously, you will have to grow into them,' she added.

'Yeah, they might fit me by the time I'm twenty,' Mac said as he pulled the trousers above his nipples.

'Nonsense.' She folded the rest of her selections. 'You go and get changed while I pay.'

Mac realised too late that the changing room he walked into was occupied. 'Sorry... Oh, it's you.'

The Suit. He beckoned Mac in before pulling the curtain behind him closed. They stood nose to nose.

'Um, can I help you with something?'

'Yes,' said The Suit. 'You can explain what happened last night.'

'Could you be a bit more specific?'

'Why did your tracker go offline?'

'Oh, well, Zalot misunderstood something I said and … hang on. Tracker?'

'Of course, we've been tracking you since the barn. We cannot risk that alien getting away.'

Mac picked his clothes up from the floor and examined them. 'Where is it?'

The Suit pointed to Mac's bag. Mac turned the familiar backpack over in his hands. Then he saw it – a grinning yellow emoji badge on the strap. Mac looked from The Suit to the emoji and back again. The two couldn't have looked any more different.

'You've been spying on me?'

'That's what I do,' The Suit said. 'Nothing personal, kid. The Boss is getting impatient, and I don't want to get on her wrong side.'

Mac gathered up his clothes and tore open the curtain.

The Suit put his hand on Mac's shoulder. 'You have to realise what's at stake. If it's between an invasion of your privacy or an invasion of this planet, there's no competition. You can understand that, right?'

Mac shrugged. 'What I think seems to matter very little, anyway.'

Mac waited in the doorway to the shop rather than risk getting cornered by The Suit again. That's where he found Zalot, scanning the city.

'What's the matter?' Mac was afraid of the answer.

'Where is all the green?'.

'Green? Oh, you mean trees and grass. Well, they got rid of all of that to make room for the buildings,' Mac explained.

Zalot's eye clouded over, and a fat tear splashed onto the concrete. 'But that was life!'

'I know but the people who built the city needed to make room for shops and offices. Otherwise, where would people work or go to buy things? And if trees weren't cut down, where would we get wood or paper?'

'It does not seem right to me,' Zalot said.

'No,' Mac agreed. 'It doesn't. But human beings are learning. It's always on the news. People are beginning to understand that if they keep on cutting trees down, one day, they will all be gone.'

'Yet still, they do it. They have to learn faster.'

'Zalot, don't do anything silly.'

'Not silly; something very smart.'

Again, Zalot conjured up the floating orbs. When the flashes of light touched the cold grey of the buildings, the concrete shuddered and groaned as though it were some mythical beast awakening from a deep sleep. It seemed to Mac that the building was moving, that at any moment it would kick up its foundations like a pair of heavy boots and start trundling down the main street.

It was when the first bursts of green erupted through the roof of a looming office block that Mac realised that it was not the building that was alive but what was growing from within it. All around him, vines broke through roofs, sending tiles clattering to the pavement. The local Tesco was unrecognisable below a layer of green matting. A circle of ivy encircled the top of the church clock tower like a halo.

Mac's mother joined them in the doorway. 'Goodness gracious me.' She tutted as though she were complaining about the weather. 'These plants are getting out of control again.'

'Yes, they are.' Mac scowled at Zalot.

The alien stood surveying his work with a satisfied smile.

'What is this?' yelled a furious man as he stared at the vines sealing closed his shop door. 'These lousy plants can't just choose to cover my shop. I won't have it.' He began to tear at the leaves covering the side of his building. A vein that throbbed in the side of his head threatened to burst.

'I would not do that if I were you,' Zalot said.

A vine snaked out from the building and wound itself around the man's ankle. It flipped him upside down and gave him a good shake. Coins and used hankies fell from his pockets. It then threw him across the pavement where he landed in a dazed heap.

Zalot stood with a pair of his tentacles resting on the area where his hips should have been.

'What have you done?' Mac asked.

His mother was too busy waving at a woman, who was munching on the bushes covering the Tesco store, to notice that Mac was talking to himself again. It seemed the zene particles from Zalot's last trick had not yet returned to normal.

'I have done the only sensible thing,' Zalot said. 'There was no point in me returning this city to its natural beauty just for the humans to tear it down again. I made it so that the plants could defend themselves.'

Mac watched as the woman nibbling at the bush got a slap to the rump by an offended branch.

'Stop worrying.' Zalot rested a tentacle on Mac's shoulder. 'It will all be alright in the end.'

A Lesson in Manners

In the packed carriage on his way home, Mac struggled to see the exciting new city around him. He stood wedged between a man who seemed determined to take his head off with a flailing elbow and his mother's less-than-fresh armpit. Worse, a baby sat in its buggy with a fully loaded nappy strapped to its bottom. Mac tried not to breathe.

A young man sat sprawled, his boots resting on the cushion of the seat opposite. The other passengers scowled at him as they were jostled around in the speeding train.

'Pass me another drink,' he yelled to his friend, as he squashed his empty can in his fist and threw it on the ground. 'It's boiling in here!'

Zalot had disappeared into the crowd when they had entered the carriage. It was only when Mac felt a tugging at his shirt that he realised Zalot stood behind him, his tentacles wrapped close to his body to save room.

'Mac, is that Earthling deflating?' he said with his voice full of concern.

Mac strained to look over the head of the short, balding man in front of him.

'Will you stop fidgeting?' his mother snapped, her temper beginning to fray.

Finally, Mac managed to see what Zalot was pointing to. On the other side of the carriage stood an old lady with a face that was rippled with wrinkles. Mac could see what Zalot meant. With loose skin pooled around her eyes, she did look as though somebody had let the air out of her face. With every bump of the train, she lurched forward, grasping her stick for dear life. She saw Mac looking at her and gave him a weary smile.

'No, Zalot,' Mac whispered. 'She isn't deflating. She's just old. As humans get older, their skin does that. Also, they find it more difficult to get about as their bones are not as strong as they used to be.'

'Really? Zergonians do not have this problem. All that happens as we get older is the colour of our **zeptar** changes.' Zalot pointed to the red flap of skin in the middle of his head. 'The darker it gets, the older a Zergonian is, and so the more respect they are given.'

Mac wanted to ask Zalot how old he was, but his mother had told him this was a rude question. 'I like the Zergonian way. Unfortunately, not everybody on Earth treats older people the way they deserve.'

'But you do,' Zalot said. 'I saw you helping your friend.'

Mac frowned. 'Oh, you mean Mrs O'Connor. Yes, well, neighbours should help one another. Besides, she's nice.'

Had he not been focused, Mac would have missed what happened next. Zalot did not conjure his army of floating orbs or make the world melt away before their eyes. He swished his tentacle, and one lonely globe flickered into life. It was not a pure white as it had been before but a deep pulsating red.

'What are you going to do with that?' Mac stared at the tiny speck.

'Even things up,' Zalot said with a wink. It is difficult to imagine how he winked with one eye, but Mac was sure that was what he had done.

'Why is the light red this time?'

'Well, the effects will be a little more permanent,' Zalot admitted.

Mac wasn't sure he liked the sound of that.

Zalot launched the red sphere into the air and it flew toward the woman where she stood clasping her stick. Then it rebounded and hit the young man in the leather jacket as he sat drinking from a can. It continued, ping-ponging between them. At first, Mac thought it hadn't worked and that nothing was going to happen, but then the woman stood taller, her spine uncurled, and a relieved smile crossed her face. The young man, however, griped and moaned to his friends about his various aches and pains.

'Now things are fairer. He, who did not appreciate his youth, has lost a little of it. And she, who needed it, has regained some.'

As they pulled into the station, the man struggled to get to his feet as he sat yelling at his friends for help. Nobody was paying him any attention, though.

They were busy watching the old lady as she did a cartwheel across the platform and through the exit.

The Rescue

'Stay between these two groynes.' Mac's mother was laid out on her towel, with her sun hat pulled down over her face.

Mac trotted down to the water's edge. Hands on hips, he stood admiring the view. 'Beautiful, isn't it?'

'Beautiful,' Zalot agreed.

However, he wasn't looking out to sea; he was poking at a supermarket shopping bag that had washed up on the shore. He lifted it out of the water and held it up, dripping, by a tentacle.

Before he had time to comment, Mac snapped. 'Don't start! Can't we take one day off! Do you know what you are? You're a fun sponge! You suck the fun out of everything!' He grabbed his lilo from the sand. 'I am not going to let you ruin this for me.'

Mac marched towards the surf. With just a few wobbles, he was up on his inflatable. He sprawled on his back, the rays warming him against the chilly sea. 'Perfect!'

A lone cloud drifted in the sky above him. Mac couldn't help noticing that, between its round shape and wispy tendrils, it looked irritatingly like Zalot. He squeezed his eyes shut, refusing to think about him; it was time to relax.

Seagulls squawked as they circled in the air above him. Other than that, all was quiet. *Too quiet,* Mac thought. He could no longer hear the waves breaking on the beach or the babble of picnicking families.

When Mac sat up and looked, he found that he could just about see the red of the parasol that his mum had been sunbathing under. He lay down on his belly and paddled with his arms towards the shore. His sweaty chest stuck to the hot plastic.

Mac stopped to check his progress. He was even further from the shore than he was before. He could no longer make out the spot where his mother lay. The current was taking him out to sea. He frantically paddled his arms, muscles complaining with each stroke he made.

He looked up and realised that he could no longer see the shore at all. 'Help!' he screamed. 'Help!'

His voice was hoarse by the time he gave up, realising nobody could hear him. *Don't panic, Mac,* he told himself.

Then he saw the ferry. It sliced through the water, the sea bubbling and churning at its hull. Mac knew if it got any closer, he would be sucked underneath.

'Look down here!' He yelled and waved at the passengers on the deck, but the drone of the ferry muted his cries.

'They can't hear you.'

Mac whipped around and nearly capsized his lilo. A few metres away, he saw Zalot bobbing in the water like a beach ball. 'Zalot, how… Never mind. Can you help me? Use the zene particles to part the sea or something?'

Zalot considered this for a moment, and Mac worried he was going to refuse. He knew from experience that the alien could hold a grudge.

'It might be easier if we swim,' Zalot said. He was by the lilo in just a couple of strokes of his muscular tentacles.

'I've tried. The current is too strong.'

'Maybe for two arms,' Zalot agreed, 'but not for six.'

He clamped a tentacle onto the lilo before beginning an impressive front crawl. Tentacles whirled as they dove in and out of the water.

The shoreline came into focus. 'You're doing it!'

Mac felt giddy as the beach took shape. He saw a group of teenagers playing football on the sand. A toddler ran ahead of her mum, collecting shells in a bright yellow bucket. A middle-aged man stood in thigh-high water, his belly as round as the beach ball he had waded in to retrieve. His mum was still spread-eagled on the sand. A flush of relief swept over him.

When they reached the beach, Zalot slumped down onto the sand.

'Thank you,' Mac said. 'And I'm sorry about before.'

The alien gave a solemn nod.

After they had packed up all their stuff and were heading towards the car, Mac hung back for a moment, pretending to empty a stone from his shoe. He took the chance to dig a hole in the sand. In it, he placed the smiley badge. If GAS were going to capture Zalot then they would do it without his help. It was the least that he owed him.

The Betrayal

The tree bark was spongy under their feet, yet Mac's mother had to keep steadying herself. That may have been because she was staring, hypnotised, at her smartphone.

'Don't go where I can't see you,' she said, without lifting her eyes from the screen.

Mac ran straight toward the 'Tree Top Trail.' It cut a wooden pathway through the forest. He had loved it as a kid. He supposed technically he still was one, though he didn't feel that way. He had been tiny when he had last been there. The trail had seemed enormous to him then. He had a vague memory of his father leading him onto the wooden bridge, promising him it was safe.

Mac felt nostalgic for those days as he viewed the sturdy walkways wrapped comfortably in their safety nets. Scaling it was not quite the mission, worthy of Indiana Jones, that he remembered.

Though, obviously, it was not just his age that had changed since then. He was an alien tour guide now. It made sense that everything would seem smaller to him.

Still, Mac decided the trail would have to do. Zalot would be able to see enough.

Mac glanced over at his mum, who grinned down at her phone. He took the opportunity while she was distracted and set his backpack on the ground.

Zalot popped out, shedding the empty bag as he lifted himself with his tentacles. 'This is amazing.'

'Yeah, it's nice.'

'Nice? Look at these trees!' Zalot turned himself, his body floating upon his tentacles so that they corkscrewed below him. When he had completed a couple of full turns, he pirouetted to face Mac. 'Some of these trees will have been here on our last visit, maybe even the one before that.' He swept a tentacle across the horizon. 'This is what we need to save.' He pulled in deep breaths that made his body swell as though he were being pumped up.

After spending some time admiring the view, he turned to Mac, his eyebrow raised. 'Why did you bring me here?'

'So that you could see we are protecting it. Look around you: no buildings, no traffic, no concrete.'

'Yes. But is it enough?' Zalot suckered his way across the trail, occasionally stopping to take in the view beyond.

Mac paused to look at the scenery. He wanted to feel the calm before he had to face the next storm Zalot would concoct.

When he leaned across the barrier to get a better look at a family picnicking in the clearing beyond, he saw him. It appeared that GAS needed someone to explain the 'secret' part of their job description to their secret agents.

Mac jogged to catch up with Zalot, hoping to distract him before he noticed The Suit.

He was too late; Zalot already stood looking over the barrier, his eye narrowed. 'Who was that?'

Mac pretended to strain to see what Zalot was looking at, although they had both seen the agent duck behind the tree, as clear as day. But he had never been any good at acting, and when he met Zalot's eye, it was filled with betrayal.

'You're working with them.'

'No! I mean, I knew they were following us, but I buried the tracker...' Mac stopped, knowing his excuses sounded feeble. 'I'm sorry but GAS told me about your plans for an invasion and I need to think about my family and friends.'

'GAS? An invasion?'

'Yes, Global Alien Surveillance. They said you are looking for a suitable landing point for the rest of your people. They are trying to stop it.'

'Those people,' Zalot said, jabbing a tentacle towards the crowd of suited men gathering below, 'have nothing to do with protecting the Earth. GAS indeed. They are WIND: Worldwide Industrial and Nuclear Development. All they are concerned about is how much money they stand to lose if COZI intervenes. I haven't lied to you. I am here for a tour to help me write my report, as I told you.' Zalot's words dripped with disappointment.

To Mac, it would have felt easier if Zalot had shouted at him. Or even if he had grabbed Mac by the feet and swung him above his head, like a cowboy with a lasso, before flinging him from the Tree Top Trail. 'I'm sorry. They told me I would be saving the human race.'

'You still don't understand,' Zalot said. 'Without our help, you are all doomed anyway.'

With that, Zalot crouched down, flattening himself against the wood of the walkway. At first, Mac thought he was cowering in fear, and he wanted to assure him that The Suits wouldn't hurt him. Although he realised that he couldn't promise that.

But Zalot wasn't frightened. He was preparing. The muscles in the alien's tentacles pulsed as he flexed and relaxed them. Suddenly, he was launched into the air as if on powerful springs. He latched onto a branch of the tree above and hung there for an instant.

Mac glanced down at The Suits as they rushed towards the trail.

'Take care of yourself.' Zalot swung from tree to tree before he disappeared out of view.

Several of The Suits were chasing him.

'Don't hurt him!' Mac turned on his heel and charged down the trail in the same direction.

He ran past his mother, who was sat on a nearby bench, typing furiously. 'Don't go far, Walter.'

Mac reached the 'spider's web' climbing frame as Zalot landed, spreading out his tentacles like an arachnid on the ropes. They gave a little before snapping back and propelling Zalot into the highest branches of the nearest tree. Then, he was gone.

Pick On Someone Your Own Size

It had been over a week since the trip to Moors Valley, and Mac was beginning to think he had imagined the whole thing. The Suits, who had found it so difficult to remain unseen before, had disappeared into the foliage like chameleons.

Mac had craved his own space for so long; it felt ridiculous that he was lonely. It was just him and his mum again.

'What's up, loser?'

Mac felt a shove from behind that sent him staggering forward. Ryan. He loomed over Mac. His red skin was a rash of angry freckles, each jostling for space on his upturned nose.

'Leave it out.' Mac tried to keep his tone casual as he knew from experience that Ryan loved to get a reaction from him.

'Leave it out,' Ryan repeated in a whiny voice. He tugged Mac's bag from his shoulder. 'What do you have in here, then?'

'Give it back!'

Ryan smirked at him. 'Or what? You'll tell your daddy?'

Ryan knew Mac wouldn't tell his dad about this or anything else. It was as if he had the powers of some vile supervillain and knew exactly what to say to hurt him most.

'You don't have anything to hide, do you?' Ryan began emptying the rucksack one item at a time. 'Rubbish,' he said as he pulled out school books and notepads before dropping them.

Mac gathered up his things and held them to his chest as he watched Ryan shake out the last of his belongings on the floor.

'That's it?' Ryan gave the bag a final shake.

But that wasn't it. First, one tentacle, then another, snaked from the bag.

'Zalot! Have you been in there the whole time?'

'Who are you talking to?' Ryan asked.

Both Mac and Zalot ignored him.

'Of course not.' Zalot tutted. 'I zorbed, in the same way that I did into the freezer cabinet at the supermarket. 'Anyway, I'm not sure I'm talking to you.' The alien turned away from him. Mac assumed Zalot was ignoring him, but then he saw that familiar light. 'However, if somebody is going to give you a hard time, I think it should be me, not this bully.'

Mac watched as a lonely white orb hit the heel of Ryan's shoe. It then bounced towards the alien, before blinking out of existence.

'What's happening?' The pitch of Ryan's voice rose along with his panic.

Right in front of Mac's eyes, Ryan began to shrink. Before Mac knew it, the boy, who had towered over him before, was below his shoulder, then his knee, then he was no bigger than Mac's little finger.

'What have you done to me?' Ryan squeaked as he clambered onto Mac's shoe and waved his tiny fist at him. 'I'm going to get you for this!'

Ryan's eyes widened as Zalot hoisted him up into the air and waved him around like a baby's rattle.

Mac wasn't sure which explanation Ryan would find less terrifying: that he had been shrunk and was being dangled aloft by an alien or that he was simply levitating in mid-air. He decided to tell him neither.

'He will never pick on anybody smaller than him again,' Zalot said with a smug grin.

Mac glowered at the alien.

'Oh, calm down; it will wear off in an hour. It's a shame though. I am sure plenty of people would sleep easier if Ryan disappeared.'

'Well, we can't do that,' Mac said, though secretly he was tempted. 'Put him in here.' Mac held open his rucksack.

Ryan lived only a few roads away, and Mac planned to stuff him through the cat flap on his way home.

For Ryan's sake, Mac hoped the cat wasn't about.

Being Walter

The door slammed behind them.

'I'm starving.' Mac raised his palm to Zalot. 'I don't mean that literally.

Mac's mum stepped from the doorway to the lounge, right in front of them. 'He's back then?'

'Who?' Mac asked.

'The alien.'

Mac realised his jaw was hanging open and snapped it shut. 'You can see him?' He pointed towards Zalot, who looked just as shocked as he did.

'Of course not,' she said. 'I'm not a WALTER.'

Zalot's tentacles flailed. 'You're a WALTER? Why didn't you tell me?'

'What are you talking about 'a Walter'?' Mac asked them both.

They answered at the same time, neither knowing that they were talking over the other.

'My guide,' said Zalot.

'Like your grandfather,' said Jenny.

'Wait, can we just pause for a moment?' Mac massaged his temples; he was beginning to get a headache. 'Now, Mum, how do you know about Zalot?'

'I didn't know he was called Zalot. But I did know he has been with us for the last week.'

'But how?'

'Who do you think sent you down that aisle to the freezer, as we have done on the same day every year? Zalot was a bit late.'

'I have no control over the zip roads,' Zalot said, despite the fact that she could neither see nor hear him.

Mac tried to think; had they gone to that same supermarket on that day every year? It was impossible to tell; a trip to the supermarket wasn't exactly memorable.

'How did you know he would be there?'

'Your grandfather told me the date and time. So, we went together, every year, until Zalot turned up.'

'How did grandad know?' Mac asked.

'I told you, he's a WALTER, too.'

'A Walter?'

'Worldwide Alien Liaison, Tours & Extra-terrestrial Rescue.'

Mac's jaw fell open again. 'That's why I'm called Walter?'

'Hang on a **zegan**,' Zalot interrupted. 'You are the WALTER I was supposed to meet all along? Then why do you call yourself Mac?'

'It's a nickname.' He didn't add that only he and Drew used it. 'I hate the name Walter.'

'Nonsense,' said Zalot. 'Being a WALTER is an honour you should be proud of.'

Mac's mum looked in the direction he had spoken. 'I'm pleased to meet you. Welcome to Earth. My name is Jenny,' she said a little too loudly whilst looking a foot too high. She turned to Mac. 'It's time we got moving.'

'Moving?'

'Of course. If we don't, we'll miss the council. Besides, WIND will be on the way.'

On the Run

'Put your seatbelt on. Both of you,' Jenny said. Mac snapped his into place, but she sped off before Zalot had time to figure out how it worked.

The tires complained as she screeched around the corner. Zalot bounced off one of the side windows, making his pupil spin dizzily. He braced all six of his tentacles between the ceiling, sides, and floor of the car.

'Mum, why the rush?' Mac willed his half-digested lunch to stay down.

'Do you remember what the 'r' in WALTER stands for?' Jenny asked.

'Um, rescue?'

'Exactly. WIND are on …' She paused. 'Oh, no.' Her eyes locked onto the rear-view mirror. 'They're behind us.'

Mac strained to look at the car behind. As he did so, a boxy black Volvo swerved around them. It easily matched the speed of his mum's Peugeot. Mac peered into the other car's window.

The Suit glared at him. Then, he waved his index finger towards Mac in a signal for him to pull over. Instead, Mac stuck out his tongue.

Jenny pushed down on the accelerator so that the Volvo dropped behind them. When they caught up again, The Suit held a gun. He pointed it out of his open window directly at Mac.

'Zalot, do something!' Mac ducked down in his seat.

Zalot released a tentacle from the car's roof handle. He gave it a swirl, conjuring up a white zene particle, and flicked it into the air, before grasping onto the handle again.

'Is it really necessary to go this fast?' If possible, the alien had turned several shades greener.

The zene particle bounced between every corner of the car before Mac opened the window to release it. It hit The Suit's gun. Only it wasn't a gun anymore. A hissing snake lunged at The Suit's face. He let out a high-pitched wail that seemed strange coming from the brutish agent. The Volvo swerved and smashed into a lamppost.

'Nearly there,' Jenny said.

'Where?'

'The supermarket, of course.'

Judgement Day

The spaceship was a perfect pyramid. It spun on its pinnacle as it lingered over the supermarket carpark. Suddenly, the ship came to a complete stop.

'It's beautiful,' Mac said as it pulsed in the dusk above them.

'What does it look like?' Jenny asked.

'You can't see it?'

'No.' She scanned the sky anyway.

Mac wasn't sure how to explain it. As he looked closer, he could see that it was inflating and deflating, as though the ship were alive and breathing.

Before he could explain, a fleet of black Volvos swerved into the parking lot.

'No time.' She pushed Mac in front of her as they headed for the supermarket entrance.

Zalot soon fell behind.

'Too slow,' Mac said, reaching for the alien's tentacle. He took his mother by the hand and looped the tentacle around her wrist.

She stared at it, bemused, before realising what he had done. 'Good idea.'

Mac took another of Zalot's tentacles, and they ran with the alien dangling between them.

'Get to the freezer aisle,' Jenny ordered.

The two humans ran either side of a shop assistant offering free samples. Zalot, invisible to him, knocked the tray from his hands and sent him floundering onto the floor.

'Sorry!' Mac shouted over his shoulder.

Mrs O'Connor waved at them from the cat food aisle as they passed. 'Hello, dears.'

'We'll talk later!' Jenny yelled as they scarpered past.

That is when Mac saw The Suits piling into the supermarket behind them. They spread out in different directions, guns drawn.

Jenny saw them too and sprinted out in front. In her haste, she missed the turn for the freezer aisle.

'Wait!' Mac watched as the alien was suspended between them like a tug of war rope.

Zalot grumbled as his tentacles stretched uncomfortably.

'Sorry,' she said to the blank space between her and her son.

A quick change of direction and they were there. Mac threw open the lid to the freezer.

Inside, he found nothing but frozen bags of potatoes.

'What now?' Mac asked.

The Suits appeared at either end of the aisle. They began to walk towards them.

All of a sudden, the two closest to them stopped.

'Will you get out of my way!' The men parted and stood to attention, saluting as a figure half their size pushed between them.

'Mrs O'Connor?' Mac said.

His neighbour looked much as she always did; her hair was tightly curled, and she wore her usual lilac cardigan. Her nasty scowl was new, though.

'I prefer 'Boss', actually.' She strode towards them, her walker abandoned. Mac wondered if she had ever needed it at all. 'Ten years I've been waiting; stuck playing a helpless old woman, when really I could have given the nod and had your whole family wiped from the Earth a decade ago.'

Her frosted lips were twisted into a snarl, exposing her tea-stained teeth.

'But…you can't be 'The Boss,'' Mac said.

'Why? Were you expecting some brutish man?' Her eyes narrowed. 'Come over here, and I'll show you just how brutal I can be.'

'You were our friend,' Jenny said.

'I was never your friend. Coffee mornings, soap operas, and knitting, your conversation nearly bored me to death.' A nasty grin tugged up one side of her mouth. 'And do you want to know something else? I really hate cats. They're treacherous little vermin.'

Mac thought of all the times she had invited him over to see Albert. Had that all been a ruse to get him alone?

She continued to walk towards them, The Suits flanking her on either side. More of them blocked the other end of the aisle, led by the first Suit Mac had met.

'What are we going to do?' Mac asked.

'I don't know,' Zalot said. 'COZI should be here by now.'

'I have an idea. Can I use a zene particle?'

With a flourish of a tentacle, one appeared in the air between them. Mac cupped it in his hand. He closed his eyes and focused on the change he wanted to make. Then he tossed it towards Mrs O'Connor.

It landed on one of her leather loafers, before blinking out of existence.

'Is that it? I'm afraid you are going to have to work a little harder than that.' She let out a throaty laugh that suddenly morphed into a strangled 'meow.' She grabbed at her throat. 'That was str… meow.' Holding her hands out in front of her, she watched as they curled into paws. 'Help me!' She clutched at the jacket of the man next to her.

He stepped back in horror as whiskers sprouted from her cheeks and black fur covered her skin. Her back arched as she dropped onto all fours. And with the blink of an eye, her transformation was complete. A black cat sat on the floor of the frozen food aisle.

Mrs O'Connor hissed at Mac. Then she sprinted down the aisle and bounded into the arms of The Suit.

'Boss?' he said, as he held her out in front of him.

She swiped at his face, knocking off his glasses and leaving four angry scratches across his forehead.

'Let's get you back to the office, Boss.' He tucked her under his jacket and pushed his way past the men behind him.

The remaining suits took a wary step forward.

'What now?' Jenny asked.

Mac didn't have a chance to answer.

As if at the flick of a switch, they were engulfed in a glowing circle of light. Mac could see the world outside of it, but it did not look the same. The Suits were heading right for them, but they were in slow-motion as if running through treacle.

All the colour had drained from the world. To Mac, it looked like a photograph from one of his grandfather's old albums, all shades of grey and aged sepia.

Inside the circle was another story. Zene orbs, a dazzling white, swirled and danced around them.

'Mum, are you seeing this?'

'I'm seeing it.' Her voice sounded strange, as though the back of her throat had shrunk to half the size, and she was forcing her words out. She wasn't looking at the orbs. Or even Zalot. 'Daddy.' Jenny threw her arms around the man in front of her – Mac's grandfather.

'How?' Mac asked.

His grandfather smiled at him over Jenny's shoulder before she finally released him.

'This is not the only world that the WALTERs work on,' his grandfather explained. 'It's a big universe, and there is a lot of work for COZI to do.'

'You are a part of the council?'

'When I was younger, I worked on Earth, welcoming the alien inspectors as they arrived at locations all over the world. Now, as part of the council, I travel the galaxy, examining worlds where the inhabitants seem set on self-destruction. I am one of the council, Walter, as you might be one day.'

'Mac,' his mother corrected. 'He prefers to be called Mac.'

'Mac?' His grandfather turned the name over in his mouth. 'I like it. You know, I could never stand the name Walter.'

'I knew it!' As Mac embraced his grandfather, he became aware of a strange tinkling sound. It reminded him of the bells on Santa's sleigh in the old films he had seen. An eerie light shimmered in front of them before taking on the form of a round table and seven chairs.

'They're coming,' Zalot said, his voice a whisper.

He may as well have saved his words because, as he spoke, a group of Zergonians, each all but identical to Zalot, appeared in their seats.

Mac's grandfather sat in one of the empty chairs. Two spaces remained at the table: one for Zalot and one for Mac.

'Join us,' one of the Zergonians said. The stripe on her head was a deep plum colour. Mac remembered that this meant she was the oldest. By the way each Zergonian had their eye trained on her, Mac assumed she was the leader. 'We have received the pictures you have sent, Zalot, and we have viewed them with interest.'

The Zergonian waved her tentacle, and a cylinder of light was beamed from the centre of the table. Within it was captured an image of Zalot's checklist. Mac had not seen it since they had left the farm.

'Point one: caring for other creatures.' The checklist flickered from view and was replaced by terrible images that made Mac feel ashamed. Tigers, with stripes of fire and night, sat with broken spirits behind metal bars. Baby seals lay clubbed on beaches, their blood turning the snow below them red. Mighty bears, chained, were made to dance for the entertainment of tourists. 'Well, that's a fail,' the Zergonian leader said.

'Point two: caring for this planet.' The screen was filled with images of rubbish laden streets and landfill sites bursting with waste. Pictures of traffic flickered into view, each car stood motionless, and bumper to bumper as black clouds of chemicals spilt into the air. 'Well needless to say that is another fail,' the leader said, her round head etched in a frown.

'Let's move onto point three: respect for yourselves.' Mac wanted to climb into the cold stone of his chair and disappear as visions of people stuffing junk food into their waiting mouths were shown. 'Hmmm,' the Zergonian muttered. 'Maybe we will have more luck on the last point: respect for each other.'

Pictures of war and explosions, fighting and bullying all lit up the viewer.

'I don't want to see anymore,' Mac yelled at the council. 'Fail us and get it over with!'

The Zergonian stared at him in puzzlement. 'Fail you? What makes you think we want to fail you?'

With another swish of her tentacle, the horrible images disappeared and were replaced with pictures of Mac himself. First, there was an image of him picking up litter outside his school. Then, he was arguing with Zalot when he feared Miss Pendell might be harmed. He saw himself placing Ryan through the cat flap (making sure the cat was nowhere around first, of course), showing him kindness despite everything the bully had done. Finally, he saw himself running with his mother, Zalot dangling between them as they tried to escape The Suits.

'We were not trying to fail you. We sent Zalot to see if the planet had hope. Paragraph nineteen, clause twelve of the Zergonian charter: No planet with hope shall be wiped clean without its inhabitants being allowed a chance to change their ways first. You humans never read the small print,' the Zergonian explained with a sigh. 'For now, the human race is safe. However, changes need to be made. It is unfortunate that such a huge responsibility will fall upon someone so young, but it is your generation that will need to save this planet.'

With a swish of her tentacle, the beam of light disappeared.

'We have seen enough. Zalot, say your goodbyes, we are going home.'

With that, the council and all its members disappeared.

'So that's it? We're going to be OK?'

'I cannot answer that,' Zalot said. 'But what I do know is that people like you bring hope to this planet. Do not ever think that you cannot make a difference.'

Zalot flashed him a gummy grin. 'Catch,' he said as he knocked a swirling zene particle out of its orbit and towards Mac.

When he caught it, Mac could feel a pulsating heat radiating from the orb. 'When we are gone, throw that as hard as you can at the floor,' Zalot instructed. 'Goodbye, Mac.'

Mac could see one last waving tentacle as Zalot was consumed by the light. Then he was gone.

Just Mac's grandfather remained.

'Will I see you again?' Mac asked.

His grandfather nodded. 'I will be back to check on you from time to time. After all, you have the family name to live up to.' The bright lights began to circle him, and he started to fade. 'And I expect to be impressed.'

'You will be,' Mac promised as his grandfather disappeared.

He and his mother were left standing together in that strange light.

'Are you ready?' His mother wiped away a tear and forced a smile.

'I'm ready.'

The Suits, who were caught in their slow-motion prison, encircled the mother and son.

Mac slammed the orb toward the ground, shattering it into a million pieces. The glittering fragments drifted around the men.

Then, The Suits started to move backwards. At first, it was at the same sluggish pace, but then they accelerated, reversing the journey they had made into the supermarket. Mac whipped round to see if Mrs O'Connor was there, but if her transformation from human to cat had been reversed, he had missed it.

It didn't stop there. Shoppers, holding baskets or pushing trollies, each trotted backwards as they made their way across the store. Shadows seemed to stretch and unwind before snapping back, repeating the same process several times over.

'Mum, what's going on?' But when Mac turned to her, she was gone. 'Mum!' Surely COZI would not have been cruel enough to take her with them and leave him alone.

'Walter, will you move yourself!' came his mother's voice from the other end of the aisle.

A few paces away, a woman pushing a whining toddler in a stroller, eyed him suspiciously.

Mac realised that COZI had turned back time to before the inspection had happened.

A fogged-up freezer cabinet stood in front of him. Mac flipped open the lid. It was empty, except for bags of chips and potatoes.

The inspection was over.

'If you want something done…' his mother muttered, reaching in for the chips.

…*you have to do it yourself*, Mac thought. That was what he planned to do. There was much to be done, and Mac could not wait to get started.

The Zergonian Language from Z to Z

Zanbot
A translating device worn in the form of a bracelet.

Zanolve
A machine that wipes memories. Must only be used by an expert.

Zapna
The only source of food on Zergon. It is taken from the Zergon sea giraffe. It is frozen at very low temperatures, a little like Earth's ice cream, but it is tasteless.

Zarno
A transmission system that allows information to be translated from the ship's central computer, directly into a Zergonian's brain, at the twist of a knob.

Zaynap
A ball made of energy generated by zene particles. Allows the user to travel in space without a suit.

Zebde
A nerve.

Zeflar
A joke or a laugh.

Zegan
A Zergonian unit of time. It can be manipulated at an individual's will to be as short as a second or as long as a year.

Zene	The particles which are the building blocks for all life and existence.
Zenta	A Zergonian's limbs.
Zeptar	A spike of skin on the top of the head, which darkens in colour as a Zergonian ages.
Zergon	A small planet five hundred light-years from the Milky Way. It has three suns and no moon. The atmosphere is similar to that of Earth.
Zergonian	A being from the planet Zergon. Also, the language spoken by all inhabitants of Zergon.
Zet	Equivalent to twenty Earth years.
Zip way	An intergalactic highway for spaceships. Please be aware, toll charges apply.
Zorbing	A Zergonian method of transportation in which the zene particles of a thing or person are separated, allowing it to travel safely at light speed.
Zuznic	A beetle which eats the bodily waste of the Zergonian people. Also used as an insult.

Made in the USA
Monee, IL
12 October 2020